PLEASE HELP ME, GOD

We Have a New Baby!

Christine Harder Tangvald

Illustrated by Benton Mahan

Chariot Books

David C Cook Publishing Co

Dedicated to my husband, Roald,
And to Rolf, Thor, Leif, and Rondi Tangvald;
Four of the cutest babies ever created.
Good job, God!
Thanks.

Chariot Books is an imprint of David C. Cook Publishing Co.

David C. Cook Publishing Co., Elgin, Illinois 60120
David C. Cook Publishing Co., Weston, Ontario

WE HAVE A NEW BABY!
© 1988 by Christine Harder Tangvald for text and Benton Mahan for illustrations.

Cover and interior design by Dawn Lauck

First Printing, 1988
Printed in Singapore
96 95 94   9 8 7 6 5

Library of Congress Cataloging-in-Publication Data

Tangvald, Christine Harder
   We have a new baby.
   (Please help me, God)
   Summary: Advice for the big sister or brother when a new baby arrives. Includes what babies can or can't do, how to help parents, and dealing with resentment and jealousy.
   1. Brothers and sisters—Juvenile literature. 2. Infants—Juvenile literature. 3. Brothers and sisters—Religious life—Juvenile literature. [1. Brothers and sisiters. 2. Babies] I. Mahan, Ben, ill. II. Title. III. Series: Tangvald, Christine Harder. Please help me, God.
BF723.S43T33 1988   155.4'43   87-35457
ISBN 1-55513-503-X

We have a new baby in our family! We do!

Our new baby has a name. It is ＿＿＿＿＿＿＿＿＿＿.
Isn't that a great name?

I have a great name, too. It is ＿＿＿＿＿＿＿＿＿＿.
I like having my very own name.

A baby is a miracle from God. When I was a new baby, I was a miracle from God. I was tiny and wonderful and special.

I'm not tiny anymore, but GUESS WHAT! I am still *wonderful* and *special.*

I really am.

God has a special plan for every single baby. He knows *exactly* how He wants each person to be.

I am the ONLY person exactly like me. God made me wonderful and different from anyone else in the whole world.

I am a ☐ boy ☐ girl.

God gave me eyes that wink and blink. He gave

me arms that swing and _____

and feet that run and _____.

I am this tall: _____.

I weigh _____ pounds.

Something really special or different about me is

_____.

My mom and dad love me just the way I am. So does God. You see, God made me *just right!*

God made our new baby wonderful, too—different from anyone else in the whole world.

Our new baby is a ☐ boy ☐ girl.

And our new baby has _____ fingers that point, and _____ toes that wiggle and squirm.

Our new baby is _____ inches long and weighs _____ pounds, _____ ounces.

Something really special or different about our new baby is _____.

Mom and Dad and I love our new baby. So does God. You see, God made our new baby *just right*.

Lots of families have new babies. Some other kids I know who have new babies in their family are:

1. _____

2. _____

3. _____

Did you know God's babies come in lots of colors? They do.

Ann's new baby brother is the color of rich chocolate, and he has lots of dark, curly hair.

Beth's and Brian's baby sister is the color of vanilla ice cream, and she has light, blonde hair.

Jeff's new brother is the color of honey, and he doesn't have any hair at all yet!

And Joey's family just adopted two babies— TWINS! They're the color of smooth caramel, and both of them have lots and lots of straight, black hair.

I am the color of _____ ,

and I have _____ hair.

Our new baby is the color of _____ ,

and has _____ hair.

Yes, God made each one of us *exactly* the way He wants us to be . . . Beeeeeeautiful!!

The Bible even says so:

For you created my inmost being; you knit me together in my mother's womb. I will praise you because I am fearfully and wonderfully made; your works are wonderful, I know that full well.

(Psalm 139:13,14, NIV)

Brand-new babies are really tiny and they sleep a lot. Sometimes new babies are a little wrinkled, but that's OK because the wrinkles go away.

Did you know that new babies can't see very well?

Sometimes babies cry a lot. Crying is their way to say, "I need you!"

And new babies don't have any teeth, yet!

These things will change in time. It's part of God's plan.

But new babies can hear,
and feel,
and kick,
and yawn,
and smile,

and _____ ,

and _____ ,

and _____ .

And wow, can they EAT!

Suck, suck!

Drink, drink!

So fast that they swallow some air. Then—pat, pat, pat—gently on the back. And . . . *B-U-R-P*! Up comes the air.

I like to feel the baby's little hand wrap around my finger and squeeeeeze!

And I like to watch the baby _____ .

My mom showed everybody a picture of ME when I was a new baby.

Guess what! I was cute, too. I was really little, and I didn't have any teeth either.

We have to DO lots of things for our new baby.
We feed the baby.
We change the baby's diapers.
We hold and rock the new baby.

We _____ .
And every day we bathe the baby. KICK AND
SPLASH! I like *my* bath, too. In fact, I love my bath.

New babies need a lot of LOVE.

God loves our new baby. So does Mom. So does Dad.

But GUESS WHAT! They still love ME, too. Just as much as ever. Maybe even *more* than ever, because being a big brother or sister is *important.* I'm getting more grown up all the time.

And there is PLENTY of love for everybody. It's like when Grandma and Grandpa come to visit. Then there are more people to love.

And the more people there are to love, the more love there is for people! That's just the way families are.

Some people who love me lots and lots are:

1. _____

2. _____

3. _____

And guess what else? I love our new baby, too. Lots and lots.

Sometimes I have different FEELINGS about having our new baby.

Mostly they are *good* feelings. I feel happy and warm. I like our new baby. I *love* our new baby. I feel proud when I show our baby to my friends.

But once in a while, I get a feeling that makes me feel bad or sad.

Once I felt angry because everybody just talked about the new baby all the time. And Mom and Dad were always busy doing something for the new baby. I wanted to say, "Hey! Look at ME! I'm still here, REMEMBER?"

But later, I got *my turn* with Mom and Dad, too. Now I know there are special times for *both* me and the new baby. Then I felt better.

Here are some feelings other kids had when they got a new baby in their family:

proud, happy, warm, gentle, loving, caring, sharing

worried, jealous, angry, lonely, tired

Have you ever had any of these feelings?

IT's OK to have different feelings when a family gets a new baby.

And its OK to TALK about how I feel. My mom and dad understand, and God understands.

I feel better when I talk about my feelings.

Since I am so big now, there are lots of things I can do to HELP with the new baby. You see, new babies make a lot of work!

1. I can carry things from the kitchen or bedroom when my mom needs them.
2. I can answer the door or the telephone very nicely. I can say, "Hello, this is _____ speaking. May I help you?"
3. I can put things away when my mom asks me.
4. And I can _____.

Another way I can help is to be very quiet when Mom and the baby are sleeping.

Sometimes that is hard to do because I think it is fun to be LOUD—to laugh and yell and run and play.

But sometimes we all have to be quiet around our new baby.

SHHHHHHHHhhhhhh.

Not *all* the time. Just sometimes.

That's when I color pictures or read or watch TV or _____ or _____ .

It's not all *that* hard to be quiet—for a little while. I can do that. Easy!

And new babies take a lot of TIME.
   —A lot of my time.
   —A lot of Mom's time.
   —A lot of Dad's time.
   WHEW!
But there are lots of things I can do to stay busy
by myself.

1. I can draw a picture of our family. See, I'm the
   one smiling the most.
2. I can practice reading books by myself so I can
   read them out loud when the baby gets bigger.
3. I can snuggle up with a warm afghan and a soft
   pillow and watch my favorite TV program.
   Maybe I can make my own TV box to sit in.

4. And I can _____.

I can also play PRETEND GAMES to stay busy.

1. I can pretend I am the king or queen of a huge country. I can make a crown out of colored paper and decorate it with jewels.
2. I can pretend I own a store and make play money and sell things to my friends.
3. I can pretend I am a mother or father, and my doll's my new baby. I can dress the baby, feed the baby, love the baby—and EVERYTHING!
4. I can pretend I am giving an important speech to lots and lots of people—right in front of my own mirror. . . . "Ladieeeees and Gentlemen!"

5. And I can pretend ＿＿＿＿＿＿＿＿＿＿.
Pretending is FUN!

Being a *big* brother or sister is an IMPORTANT thing to be.

Yes, it is! It makes me feel proud to be big.

New babies don't know very much about this world, yet. But I know lots of things because I am growing up!

I know how to work.

I know how to help.

And I know how to love.

I also know how to be soft and gentle and careful with our new baby.

Another thing I know is _____.

Yes, being a *big* brother or sister is a VERY IMPORTANT THING TO BE!!

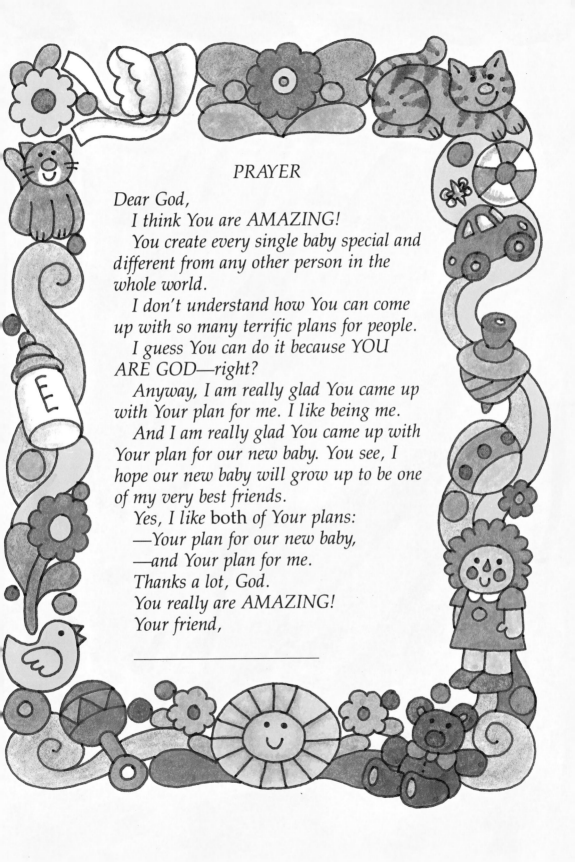

PRAYER

Dear God,

I think You are AMAZING!

You create every single baby special and different from any other person in the whole world.

I don't understand how You can come up with so many terrific plans for people.

I guess You can do it because YOU ARE GOD—right?

Anyway, I am really glad You came up with Your plan for me. I like being me.

And I am really glad You came up with Your plan for our new baby. You see, I hope our new baby will grow up to be one of my very best friends.

Yes, I like both of Your plans:

—Your plan for our new baby,

—and Your plan for me.

Thanks a lot, God.

You really are AMAZING!

Your friend,

_____

But Jesus called the children to him and said,
"Let the little children come to me."
(Luke 18:16a, NIV)

SUGGESTIONS FOR PARENTS

1. **Unconditional Love**
   All people need to be loved—to feel valuable and wanted. Show your older child through words and actions that you love him just the way he is—*unconditionally*!

2. **Physical Reassurance**
   Physical reassurance of your love is especially important right now. Hug your child. Comb his hair. Tuck him into bed. Wink at him.
   These small physical assurances can be almost as important as what you say.

3. **Familiar Schedule and Routine**
   Disrupt the older child's life as little as possible. Keep his routine and surroundings as familiar as you can (same bed and bedtime, same sitter, etc.).

4. **Small Presents**
   Wrap and stash away a few small presents for the older child (bubbles, storybook, ball, flashlight, color book and crayons, etc.). An unexpected gift is a delightful way to say, "I think you are special."

5. **Self-esteem**
   By increasing your child's self-esteem, you can reduce feelings of inadequacy and resentment that lead to jealousy. If a child has faith in himself, he will get along better with others.
   Try to create opportunities for your child to feel successful and self-confident. Praise your child as often as possible, especially when everyone is constantly bragging on the new baby.

6. **Avoid Comparisons**
   God made each child unique. When parents compare children, they make a serious mistake.
   Instead of comparing your children, celebrate their differences—the unique qualities and strengths of each child.

7. **Natural Feelings**
   It's normal and natural for an older child to have all kinds of feelings and questions when a new baby is born. Feelings need to be acknowledged and brought out into the open.
   Make sure the child has a doll or stuffed animal to talk to. Roleplaying is an excellent avenue to vent feelings.

8. **Set Limits**
   Children need limits; children want limits. Though the older sibling should be allowed to express his feelings openly, aggressive behavior needs to be controlled. The baby must be protected, especially from a toddler who might not realize the consequences of his actions.

9. **Exclusive Time**

   If possible, give your child at least a small bit of *exclusive* time and attention. Each child needs some special time alone with each parent—preferably on a regular basis. Allow the older child to be the center of your attention, even if it is just for a few minutes.

   Read a favorite story, make an ice-cream cone, challenge him to a race, let him join you on your bed for a nap, hug the child, etc. Don't always talk about the baby. A small bit of personalized time goes a long way to defray jealousy and resentment.

10. **Relax and Enjoy**

    All you can do is the best you can do. Don't forget to relax and enjoy this special time. Savor these moments with your new baby and with your older child. This exact moment will never come again.

Please go hug your children twice, *right now:*
    —once for you, and
    —once for me.
God bless.

Christine Harder Tangvald